BAD KITTY
Searching for SANTA

NICK BRUEL

ROARING BROOK PRESS
New York

Kitty wants to write a letter.
But not just any letter.
Kitty wants to write a letter to **SANTA**.

She hopes Santa will give her a nice present.

Have you been good this year, Kitty?

Kitty is not so sure she's been good this year.

Kitty writes the letter anyway.

Do you want to mail the letter, Kitty?
No. Kitty does not want to **MAIL** the letter.

Kitty wants to **GIVE** the letter to Santa!

We'd better hurry, Kitty.
That store closes soon.

Kitty can't wait to meet Santa!

I don't think that's Santa, Kitty.
Santa has a beard.

So many Santas.

Kitty doesn't like that there are so many Santas.

They're not trying to trick you, Kitty.
They just love Santa. **EVERYONE** loves Santa!

We're almost at the store, Kitty.
Now you will meet
SANTA!

I'm sorry,
Kitty.
We're too
late.

Let's go home, Kitty. You still have lots of presents to open, even if none of them are from Santa.

Sweaters.
All of Kitty's presents are sweaters.
Kitty does not like sweaters.

Kitty does not like Santa.

But Santa likes Kitty.